Face Off

Chris Forsyth

James Lorimer & Company, Publishers
Toronto, 1996

James Lorimer & Company Ltd. acknowledges with thanks the support of the Canada Council and the Ontario Arts Council in the development of writing and publishing in Canada.

Cover illustration: Ian Watts

Canadian Cataloguing in Publication Date

Forsyth, Chris
Face off

(Sports stories)
ISBN 1-55028-533-5 (bound)
ISBN 1-55028-532-7 (pbk.)

I. Title. II. Series: Sports stories (Toronto, Ont.).

PS8561.06966F32 1996 jC813'.54 C96-931864-2
PZ7.F66Fa 1996

James Lorimer & Company Ltd., Publishers
35 Britain Street
Toronto, Ontario
M5A 1R7

Printed and bound in Canada

Contents

To Chell Stephen and Zack Anderson,
inspiration on ice.

1

Blades of Steel

S*mack!* It's the sound of the puck hitting my stick that means hockey to me. Not the cheers of my dad and mom in the stands, not the yelling of my teammates, not the slashing of my skates on the ice. It's that thud when the wood and the rubber connect. That's hockey.

When I've got a hold of that puck I know I'm in control and everything is working just great. And on that Sunday afternoon in January, things couldn't have been better. Zack and I were Ice Masters Supreme. Never in a million years would I have guessed that two best friends like Zack and me would end up as enemies.

Let me introduce myself. I'm Mitch Stevens. I'm thirteen and I play centre for the A-line on the Hillcrest Stingers, a Toronto Pee Wee team. My dad, Joe Stevens, says I could skate before I could walk. I must have inherited my ability from him, because Dad played junior hockey. He could have made it to the NHL if he hadn't wrecked his knee.

My best friend, Zack Andermann, plays on the Stingers with me. We've been on a line together ever since learn-to-play when we were only five years old, with Zack playing right wing and me at centre. He's only an inch or two taller than me, but he's a lot bigger. And he can really skate! I think I'm pretty fast, but Zack's even faster. We make great plays together, with me setting things up for Zack to go in for the kill. So there we were, buddies and linemates, but things were about to change.

"Stevens and Andermann against Wolsky and Levitt." Coach Fanshawe pointed to the ends we should take, as Johnny Wolsky grumbled his way onto the ice. Wolsky is the biggest guy on our team, but he's also the slowest. He plays pretty fair defence as long as he doesn't get caught in the wrong end. Wolsky had never won a two-on-two against Zack and me all season. We weren't about to let it happen now. As we skated to our end, Zack grabbed me from behind by the numbers on my jersey. I skated hard, dragging him along as he whispered in my ear, "What do you bet Johnny never gets near the puck?" We laughed out loud, turned and stared our opponents down.

Zack swooped in from the left, scooping the puck dropped by Assistant Coach Minelli. A perfectly timed lateral pass slid over to me a nano-second before Zack deked around Johnny Wolsky. With a quick nod to Zack, I accelerated straight at Mark Levitt, locking eyes with him. I still had the puck. Johnny was puffing along behind Zack like a caboose. My eyes were clamped on Mark, but I could still see Zack zoom up on the wing. Snapping my head around in his direction, I forced Mark's eyes off me. Without breaking stride I faked him right, spun left and came out behind him in the clear. It was a tricky angle so I pushed the puck ahead for Zack to make the shot. He slammed the puck so hard it hit the net halfway up, stretching it way out in back. The net snapped the puck back onto the ice, where it landed right at our feet.

Zack took a run at me, helmet down, stick sweeping the ice in front. I lowered my head and braced for the butt. We cracked heads, raising our sticks high in the air. Like Dragon-slayers we crossed lances and had begun our finale when Coach Fanshawe blew his whistle.

"Show's over, boys. Get off the ice." Coach was pretty gruff, but I knew he was happy with our play. "Friesen and Tesma against Lee and Dunn." The next foursome took their places. I leaned over the boards to watch our linemate, Dustin Lee, show some cool moves of his own.

On that snowy Sunday afternoon, we were almost halfway through the season. The Stingers were duking it out near the top of the league. The toughest competition that year was a team from North York, the Rangers. We had a game against them later in the day. When Coach Fanshawe whistled the end of the practice, the team spilled onto the ice for some "wilding," a free period when we race around zigging and zagging, whooping, hollering and having a ton of fun.

"Everybody off the ice!" Coach Fanshawe bellowed louder than an arena full of parents. "Save your energy for the game!" Zack likes to be the first one off the ice, but I always hang back for a little swing around, just like the stars on Hockey Night in Canada. I skate out with my head down, raise my stick in the air in a salute to my imaginary fans and enjoy the imaginary applause.

Don't get me wrong; it's not like I think I'm some hotshot. Actually, I don't score a lot of goals. Zack's our top goal scorer. I get a lot of assists, but mostly I work the puck from the ends so the better shooters can get set up in front of the net. It works out pretty well for my line and because Zack is my friend, he always shares the glory when he nails one.

After practice we had only three hours before we had to be at the North York arena to face our rivals, the Rangers. Zack's dad drove us from St. Mike's arena at Bathurst and St. Clair to my house, where my mom had dinner waiting. Zack and I live just far enough apart to go to different schools.

"Give 'em heck, boys!" Mr. Andermann said as he dropped us off. He always says that. Zack told me his grandfather Andermann says it too. We laughed as he drove away.

Dumping our gear in the front hall, Zack followed me into the kitchen. My mom, Penny, was ripping a head of lettuce at the counter. Her red sweatshirt was the brightest thing in our big white kitchen.

"Hi, Mosh, what's for nosh?" I said cheerfully, peering into a bowl on the counter. I liked standing beside Mom. It felt good to know that I was already taller than her.

"Salad. Hi Zack." Mom handed us each a bottle of salad dressing from the fridge.

"Salad's not food! We need carbs: pasta and stuff. Like the pros." I picked up a leaf of lettuce from the bowl. "See this? If we don't eat carbs we'll wilt like this lettuce."

Mom laughed as she lifted the lid of a big pot on the stove. The magic aroma of spaghetti sauce wafted over us.

"All right!" Zack high-fived my mom.

Dad strolled into the kitchen, sniffing the air like a bloodhound. As he leaned over to look into the spaghetti pot, the lights reflected off his shiny bald spot.

"Hat trick tonight, Zack?" Dad asked as he straightened up, almost hitting his head on the hanging rack over the stove.

"I don't know, Mr. Stevens. If I'm gonna get a hat trick I'd like it to be on a night my dad can be there." Zack didn't fool anybody. He'd take a hat trick any time.

"We'll videotape the game. Just in case." Dad winked at me. We already had a room full of videos of our games. You need a pretty strong stomach to watch them, though. Dad waves the camera around like mad, cheering and shouting. We've got amazing footage of practically every arena ceiling in Toronto.

An hour before game time we piled our gear into Dad's van and headed out for North York. Thirty minutes later Dad pulled up to the arena doors. Zack and I hopped out and dragged our equipment out of the back of the van.

"I'm going ahead to get my skates sharpened. See you in there." With that Zack took off.

I slung my bag over my shoulder and leaned down to pick up my stick. Out of nowhere something hit me, knocking me onto the snow-covered pavement. "Hey!" I looked up to see an enormous girl, dressed all in black, carrying two bulging hockey bags. She ignored me completely. Angrily I snatched up my bag and charged after her. I felt a hand on my shoulder. "Let me get the door for you." My dad opened the door and walked with me to the dressing room. I looked around for the girl, but she had disappeared.

The dressing room was packed with players and parents when we entered. I found a spot on the bench beside Zack as Coach Fanshawe and Assistant Coach Minelli checked off names on the roster sheet. A couple of times the coach tried unsuccessfully to get everyone to quiet down. Finally, he just blew his whistle. It echoed loudly in the little room. Everyone suddenly shut up.

"I have an important announcement to make, so everybody pay attention. This summer there's going to be a special hockey camp held in Muskoka. The top twenty-five players in our league, selected by a panel of coaches at the end of the season, will go to the camp for two weeks of intensive training with some pretty well-known NHL players as guest coaches. Those twenty-five kids will then participate in a select league, playing against kids from all over Canada in a big tournament next year."

The room erupted as everybody started asking questions at once. I looked at Zack. He looked at me. A big grin spread across his face. "Muskoka, here we come," he said with his usual self-confidence. I couldn't wait to get on the ice.

Coach Fanshawe whistled us back to earth. We still had a game to play. Buzzing with excitement, we filed eagerly onto the ice. I headed for the face-off circle. As I moved into position, I found myself head-to-head with the girl who had knocked me down outside the arena. She was the centre for the Rangers!

A wicked smile on her face, she ducked down to fight for the puck, but I came up with it. I didn't have much time to enjoy my triumph because Zack was already across the blue line angling for a shot on net. I raced into position for the rebound. Rangers were stuck on Zack like flies. They forced him into the boards, but the puck scooted out onto the stick of my arch enemy, Ranger Girl. No way she was going to get through me! She faked a pass to the right. Of course I knew she was going to fake. I took a step left as she made her move. Suddenly off-balance, she let the puck loose for a mere second. It was enough for me. I had the puck in a flash and slid it in a smooth arc around the front of the net where Zack was waiting. It all took about three minutes from the time the ref dropped the puck. Stingers one, Rangers zip.

We filed back to the bench, and the B-line took the ice. Coach Fanshawe's face was already bright red. "Play your positions!" he yelled. Coach Fanshawe yelled a lot. "Stevens!"

I jumped up. "Sir?"

"Nice work. Keep playing your man."

Ha! Hadn't he noticed my man was a girl? I was thinking maybe the amazingly tall Ranger Girl could use a penalty to cool her off. Unfortunately, while I was thinking that, the Rangers scored. There is probably no worse sound than a bunch of parents from the opposing team cheering and stomping and yelling. I looked over at my dad. He gave me a thumbs up.

On our next shift, we got all tangled up as we rushed around, trying to regain the lead. At one point our defence was stuck at the wrong end of the ice when the Rangers ace scorer broke away with the puck. He screamed up the ice while we pedalled like maniacs after him. Matt Barnard, our goalie, braced himself for the attack. As the puck rocketed off the Ranger's stick, it looked for a split-second like Matt was bested. Suddenly his leg shot out, deflecting the puck into the boards. The crowd roared. It gave us the jolt that got our heads back into the game.

We were still tied when our shift ended. Zack and I begged Coach Fanshawe to let us stay on the ice.

"No way, boys." The coach was firm. "We have twenty minutes to play. Conserve your strength."

We satisfied ourselves with yelling at our teammates.

Ten scoreless minutes ticked away. Between shifts we were restless to get back out there and make something happen. When we finally returned to the ice, Zack made a breakaway that put him one-on-one with the Rangers goalie. He'd put the wood to the ice for a shot on goal when a Ranger defenceman finally caught up to him. The Ranger's stick poked at Zack's skates, tangling him up and knocking him down. Everyone jumped off our bench, screaming foul. Meanwhile, face down on the ice, Zack still had the puck and from two feet away managed to swipe his stick around the side of the net, sweeping the puck by the stunned goalie. Our screams turned to cheers! The Ranger defenceman's dumb move got him a penalty and turned the tide for our side.

Coach Fanshawe saw the light and let Zack and me stay on the ice right through the penalty. I eased into position for the face off. Mega Obnoxious Ranger Girl scowled at me. I smiled. We didn't speak. The ref dropped the disk. I wasn't smiling when MORG snatched it away. Zack was instantly on the puck in the corner. I signalled to Dustin Lee to backpedal, expecting Zack to clear the puck when he got it, which he did. Sticking to MORG like glue, I ran her off into the boards. Zack was chugging up the centre, Dustin was at the blue line and I was right behind them. Our defence was interfering nicely with the progress of the two slower Rangers. That left me, Zack and Dustin against MORG and the Rangers best forward. Zack set up outside the goal, but Dustin still had the puck, with the Ranger coming at him fast. I had MORG lumbering up on me.

Once more, she scowled and I smiled. Dustin whipped the puck over to Zack, and the Ranger changed gears, quickly following the puck. "Dusty," I shouted at Zack. I punctuated it with a hip-check that sent MORG to the ice. Zack flicked the puck back at me, but the Ranger was already heading for Dustin. The puck kissed my stick and made its way right back to Zack. The Ranger was spinning like a top. The goalie was lost in space when the puck slid under his pads. Zack lowered his head, and we went into our helmet-butting routine.

My arch enemy was sitting on the ice, shaking her head. "Polter Ice got you?" I smirked as I said it. Polter Ice is the kind that's got invisible gremlins that trip you at the worst possible moment. Okay, maybe I rubbed it in. Nobody's perfect.

2

Put Me In, Coach

Every day during the following week Zack and I talked about winning a spot on the select team. I wasn't as confident as Zack. He had the stats — tied for most goals in the league and right up there in overall points. My numbers were pretty good, but not as impressive as Zack's.

Most days we would meet after school at the outdoor rink in my neighbourhood to run practice drills and play a little pick-up with our friends. Now we had an added incentive for our extra practice. Dustin was usually there, and Matt came out when he finished practising his violin.

On this particular Friday afternoon, the four of us were sitting on the benches beside the rink, putting on our skates. Matt stood up, towering over us on his blades. Matt's incredibly tall to begin with. He looks deceptively frail with his glasses on, but put him in goal and he's lightning fast and covers a lot of net.

"My brother says there's plenty of competition out there," Matt told us. Matt's older brother was a referee in our league. "My brother says that to be one of the twenty-five kids out of all the teams, you have to be amazingly good."

"I'm going. And Mitch is coming with me," Zack said, looking up from lacing his skates. With his dark buzz-cut hair and square jaw, Zack looked as tough as his words. He had a

way of stating things that didn't leave much room for dis-
agreement.

Dustin looked at us, shaking his head. "Better not be too
cocky, Zack. Anything can happen."

Dustin was right.

But I had to agree with Zack when he said, "I'm thinking
positive. It's what you're supposed to do. Besides, don't you
guys want to go too?"

"Not me," replied Matt. "I have music camp all summer."

Zack laughed. He's not big on music. "Who makes more
money? Hockey players or violin players?"

"I don't know. And it's violinists, not violin players,"
Matt replied sharply. Matt's pretty serious about his music.

It was too cold to stand around debating. "Hey, let's just
play some hockey, okay?" I skated onto the ice. "Toss me a
puck!" Three pucks pelted me from the bleachers.

"What do you say, Dusty?" I said, skating up to our quiet
pal.

"Not much, Mitch," he replied, arranging his thick black
hair under his helmet. Dustin doesn't talk a lot, which makes
people think he's shy or something. Actually, he's a really
funny guy. He just saves it up.

After an exhilarating hour of pick-up, the sky was completely black. I was glad to be sweating from the exertion
because it was a lot colder in the darkness. We headed for
home, parting company a block from my house. A light snow
was falling as I walked the last little way. I was thinking about
what Matt's brother had said. We compete against some pretty
good Pee Wee hockey players. Kids who had even been
scouted by the pros. I wasn't sure how much of a chance we
had against them. But remembering what Zack said about
thinking positively, I told myself over and over, "You're going
to Muskoka. You're going to Muskoka."

Approaching the house, I saw a silver car parked at the curb in front. It looked exactly like Coach Fanshawe's car. I ran inside to find the coach sitting in the family room with my dad. "Hi, Coach!"

"How are you, Mitch?" Coach Fanshawe spied my skates hanging over my shoulder. "Practising for the game tomorrow?"

"Yo, I mean, yes sir," I answered.

I was pretty curious about why the coach was visiting, but nobody was talking. Finally Dad said, "Why don't you go see if you can help out in the kitchen?" That was clear enough for me. They wanted to talk about something alone. Were they already discussing the candidates for Muskoka? Close to bursting, I left and went straight to the kitchen. Mom was nowhere in sight, but my sister, Jennifer, was poking around in the pots on the stove.

"Hi, Mitch," she said. Jen is sixteen and has been playing hockey longer than I have. She plays on three teams — mixed house league, a city girls team and her high school girls team. I grabbed a handful of her long, damp hair. "Did you have a game today?"

"Yeah. We won," she replied. "Now let go of my hair."

I left Jen and snatched up the kitchen phone. Zack answered on the third ring. "Guess what? Coach Fanshawe's here." I didn't give him time to speak as I continued, "He's in the family room with my dad. They sent me out of the room."

Zack interrupted, "What do you think it's about?"

"I don't know, like I said, they sent me out of the room." At that moment my dad came into the kitchen. "Call you back." I hung up the phone hastily.

Dad opened the fridge, taking the water jug out. He put the jug on a tray with two glasses and went back into the family room. I looked at Jennifer. "Water? They're sitting around drinking water? This is really weird." It's not like my dad and Coach Fanshawe aren't friendly. They're just not *friends*, and I can't remember Coach Fanshawe ever coming to my house before. I was baffled.

It seemed like hours before they came out of that room. Dad walked the coach to the door, where they shook hands. I snuck up behind them, eavesdropping for a clue about why he was here. The second the door closed behind the coach, I nabbed Dad. "What's up?" I asked casually. For some reason my heart was pounding.

"Is your mother home yet?" Dad collected the tray on his way to the kitchen. "Let's get this dinner ready. I'm starving!"

It was clear I wasn't going to get anything out of him until he was good and ready.

By the time Mom got home from work I was starved for food and information. Zack called twice, but I put him off. Meanwhile, Dad and Jen were yakking away like nothing was unusual.

Mom walked into the dining room in her stocking feet. "Thanks for holding supper for me." Mom took her place at the table. "It smells wonderful. What's wrong with Mitch?" She looked at me and then at Dad.

"I've got a secret that Mitch is dying to know," Dad laughed.

"We don't have secrets in this family, Joe," Mom said mockingly. "Mitch looks about ready to burst. Put him out of his misery." I breathed a silent thank you to Mom.

Dad cleared his throat. "Ron Fanshawe stopped by this evening." He paused. "It seems he's being transferred to Halifax, leaving within the month." Dad looked around the table at three faces, one mildly interested, one bored and one — mine — completely riveted.

"That's nice," Mom said casually.

"Actually, Penny, the interesting thing is he wants me to take over the team."

My fork flipped off the table as I brought my hands up in surprise. "Wow, Dad!" I exclaimed. "Cool!"

Mom wasn't entirely convinced about the coolness of the idea. "Coaching's going to take a lot of time. What did you tell him?" That's my mom, the practical one.

"I told him I'd talk it over with my family." Dad looked around the table again. I had my two thumbs up. "Well, I guess that's a 'yes' from Mitch. What about you, Jen? Any opinion?" Dad looked expectantly at my sister.

"Okay by me." She shrugged.

"That leaves you, Penny." Dad turned to my mom.

She laughed as she said, "You're a big boy, Joe. You do what you think is best."

They were chuckling between themselves as I slipped away to the phone and dialled Zack's number. "Zack," I whispered when he answered, "Coach Fanshawe is leaving. My dad's going to be our coach."

"Cool," Zack exclaimed. "Your dad's going to make a great coach."

"Yeah," I said excitedly, "and think of the extra ice time we're gonna get. So we can make the select team."

"Hey, don't the coaches decide who goes to Muskoka?" Zack reminded me.

"Awesome, we've got one vote already!" I nearly shouted into the phone. "I can't wait 'til next practice. We'll be smokin'!"

"Look, I've got to go finish my homework," Zack interrupted. "I'll see you at the rink tomorrow."

As I hung up the phone I could already picture Zack and me tearing up and down the ice with Dad cheering us from the bench. I was thinking positive just like Zack said.

3

Hey, Remember Me?

The first practice with Dad coaching was the next weekend. I was pretty keen to get to the arena. Knowing how proud Dad was of me and Zack, I was certain that he would give us extra attention to help us win the competition.

We arrived at the arena early. Dad had the coach's clipboard and was going over some stuff with Mr. Fanshawe and Assistant Coach Minelli. There was another team practising on the ice so I sat and watched from the stands. They were little kids, maybe six or seven years old, all crashing into each other and falling down on the ice when they weren't even moving. It made me remember when Dad was teaching me to skate. No matter how many times I fell, Dad waited patiently for me to struggle to my feet or picked me up when I got too tired. It seemed like a long time ago, and I was really looking forward to having fun like that again.

I was so engrossed in my memories that I didn't see Zack until he jammed his helmet onto my head. "Earth to Mitch. Come in, Mitch." Zack was talking into the end of his hockey stick.

"Hey, Zack! Remember when we skated like that?" I pointed to the kids on the ice.

"No way we ever skated like that, man," he replied. "Come on," he urged. "Let's go say goodbye to Coach Fanshawe."

We climbed down the stands and headed to the dressing room while I tried to pull Zack's helmet off my head. I had never realized how much smaller Zack's head was than mine.

While we got ready, all the parents were busy saying goodbye to the coach and talking to Dad. "Everybody onto the ice!" Coach Stevens yelled.

"Yo, Dad!" I shouted.

Dad looked at me and smiled, "That's 'Yo, Coach.'"

We stampeded out onto the ice and lined up expectantly in front of our new coach. Dad looked us up and down, checked his clipboard and conferred with Assistant Coach Minelli.

Everyone was on their best behaviour, waiting quietly for Dad to give us our orders. Finally, his conference over, he looked up and down the line, smiling broadly. "Okay, kids, I want you to team up in pairs. You and your partner will race each other from one end of the ice to the other. Coach Minelli and I will be timing you. The idea is to really burn up the ice."

We immediately began picking partners. Naturally, I teamed up with Zack. Dad turned to us and said, "No, wait a minute, Zack. I'd like you to skate with Natalie here." That was so ridiculous that both Zack and I laughed out loud. Not because Natalie is a girl — the only girl on our team, in fact — but because she's strictly a B-line drone. Okay, she's nice enough, but she's quite a lot smaller and slower than the rest of the guys. With that long red braid hanging down her back, she looks like Anne of Green Gables on skates.

"Zack!" Dad snapped sharply. "Let's go!"

Zack took off, leaving Natalie in his frost. When my turn came, I was paired with James Friesen. James is no rocket either. Needless to say, I left him standing.

For the next drill we stickhandled a puck up the ice in the same pairs. Natalie and James weren't even over the blue line before Zack and I finished our runs. With these two drills finished, Dad and Assistant Coach Minelli had a little conference. I took the opportunity to have a little conference of my own with Zack, Dustin and Matt.

"Kinda like first practice, eh?" Dustin said.

"I'm sure Dad, I mean Coach Stevens, knows what he's doing," I said. "He played Junior Hockey, you know."

"We know!" they chorused.

Okay, so maybe I'd told them a few times before.

A whistle blew, bringing our attention to centre ice. "All right, kids, I'm going to call out some names and I want those players to come with me. The rest go with Assistant Coach Minelli." Dad proceeded to rhyme off the names of half of the players there. Zack was called; I wasn't. Zack gave me a puzzled look as he skated off with Dad and his group. I looked back at my group. Man, oh man, nothing but Natalie and the slowpokes. Stickhandling lightweights. What was I doing in this group of misfits? I zoomed over to the assistant coach. "Excuse me, sir," I said. "Are you sure I'm in this group?"

Mr. Minelli didn't even check his sheet. "You sure are, Mitch," he replied. "Let's get down to the other end. Come on, kids." With that he skated off, leaving me completely speechless.

I shrugged and followed the group. "Stevens, Plaxton and Friesen, you face off against Rothenberg, Tesma and Dunn." Assistant Coach Minelli waved Nick Russell into goal. "We'll be working the corners, so don't be afraid to go after the puck." He paused, looking at me. "Ready?"

I wheeled into position for the face off. Opposite me, Ian Rothenberg gave me a goofy smile.

"Hey, Ian." I smirked.

Assistant Coach Minelli dropped the puck. Ian was still smiling his goofy smile, and I had the puck out of there before he woke up. Natalie missed the pass out completely. Assistant Coach Minelli guided the puck behind the net. "Get back there!" he shouted. We all sprang into action. Six bodies converged on the puck, flailing and slashing. I was able to get my stick on it first, blasting it out off the boards for a defenceman to pick up. Of course nobody was there. Eventually Natalie got to the puck and started looking around. I was set up perfectly in front of the net, shouting at her. She promptly shovelled the puck to Ian, who, amazingly, popped it into the goal. "Nat Plax, you goof!" I screamed. "He's on the other side!"

Assistant Coach Minelli interrupted me. "Good pass, Natalie. That's what we're looking for. Stevens, settle down."

For the next thirty minutes we practised digging out from the corners, setting up shots on goal and making passes on the fly. It seemed to me that I had to do everything — set it up, get things going. Apparently nobody noticed that I was doing all the work. It took the entire half-hour just to get James Friesen to make a decent backhand pass.

At the first break in the action I sailed over to Dad, who was deep in conversation with Assistant Coach Minelli. "Dad," I interrupted, "can I talk to you?"

"Not now, Mitch." He didn't even look at me, just kept talking to the assistant coach. I waited awkwardly for a few moments, then skated around to cool off. As soon as I saw them move apart, I zoomed back over to my dad.

"Dad?"

He looked up from his clipboard. "Yes, son?" His expression was stern, as if I was bothering him or something.

"Why did you stick me with the wheezers?" I demanded.

"The *what*?" he said, his voice rising.

"You know, the slowpokes, Natalie and James. Why aren't I with Zack and Dusty?"

"Mitch, I don't want to hear you call your teammates 'wheezers,' or any other name for that matter. We're all working together here to develop our skills. Everybody is an equal member of this team."

I couldn't think of a response to that, so after a few seconds of staring at Dad I just went back to my wheezer teammates.

By the time the whistle ended practice, I was completely steamed. My friends in the other group were laughing and talking like they'd just had the time of their lives. In fact, the kids in my group were also laughing and talking. Was I the only one who thought something was terribly wrong?

For the first time ever, I didn't feel like making my star turn. I left the ice, silently filing into the dressing room. I sat down beside Zack, waiting for him to say something. Finally he noticed me sitting there. "Mitch, we missed you on the line. How'd it go at your end?"

"Don't ask," I grumbled. "I was on a line with Natalie Plaxton."

Zack grinned at me.

"Knock it off. It's not funny," I glowered at him.

"Lighten up, Mitch. It's just practice. Next game we'll be back on the line together, rackin' up goals. One step closer to you-know-where." As usual, Zack's mind was on the future, and he said just the right thing to remind me of our goal.

"Thanks, buddy," I said, easing up a bit.

I bantered back and forth with the guys outside the dressing room for a while. One by one, they took off with their folks, leaving me alone to wait for my dad, *Coach* Stevens. I was feeling okay until Dad came out of the dressing room. Then it all came back to me, the humiliation of being separated from my friends and my line, of being in the B-group with Natalie and James. I figured anybody could see that I was mad. Instead my dad came out of the dressing room with a big smile on his face, like nothing at all was wrong.

"Good practice, eh Mitch?" he said heartily, picking up my bag.

I was flabbergasted. Good practice? For who? I followed him out of the arena and sat in the van without saying a word. He should have known.

4

Hardball at the Software Company

"Look at this, Mitch, a whole Sunday with no hockey games or practice. How about joining your old dad for a day at the office?" my father said, as he poured orange juice into two glasses.

I wasn't too keen on spending the day with my dad, the traitor, so I just shrugged. A maybe-yes-maybe-no shrug. He could take it whichever way he wanted. After yesterday's humiliation on the ice I wasn't yet ready to forgive and forget.

"Toast?" he inquired.

I pretended I didn't hear him, just to tick him off.

"Mitch," he persisted, "wake up, Mitch." He fired me a quizzical look.

"I thought I'd spend some time with Zack today, Dad," I said, figuring that would get him off my back. No such luck. He swung around and picked up the phone, dialling a number from memory.

"Fred! Hello, it's Joe. I'm taking Mitch into the office shortly and he'd like Zack to come along." Dad paused, listening to Mr. Andermann's reply. He turned a zillion-watt smile on me, all smug and happy. "That's great. No, we'll pick him up in about ten minutes. See you then." He hung up the phone. "Well, grab your coat, Mitch. Zack's waiting!"

I slunk out of the kitchen, scowling. Now he thinks he's the coach of my spare time, I thought. At least I would have Zack on my side, so the day wouldn't be a total loss.

My Dad's company makes really cool educational software. It's called interactive learning because it lets you play computer games to improve your skills instead of just looking at pictures and words. Any other time I would've jumped at the chance to spend the day at his office. He uses me as a guinea pig, checking out the systems from a kid's perspective. This makes sense, considering the computer programs are created for kids to use. Dad and his partner, Sheldon Kates, let me try out the stuff, and then we sit down and have what Dad calls a debriefing session. Sometimes the stuff I test doesn't get released. Other times they actually use some of my suggestions. I even have my name on some of the company's CD-ROMs.

After picking Zack up, Dad drove down Christie and turned onto Davenport Road. We drove past Casa Loma, an enormous castle where nobody lives that's full of tourists walking around. It's weird having tourists in your hometown — it's not like Toronto is Disneyworld or anything.

As we headed downtown, Dad announced, "We are now passing Maple Leaf Gardens, home of the …" Dad paused, "what's the name of that hockey team, again?" Zack and I looked at each other and rolled our eyes. I kept my mouth shut, but Zack finally mumbled, "I think they're called the Leaves or something." What a couple of comedians. I was embarrassed for both of them.

When we got to the office, Sheldon was already there. "Hi, fellas," he greeted us. "Glad you could come and help us out today."

"Shel, you remember Mitch's friend, Zack," Dad said.

"Sure, I do," he replied. "I hear you're the star player on the hockey team." Zack was so busy beaming he didn't notice my jaw hit the floor. Star player? Yeah, so what does that make me, the moon?

I was still smarting from that remark as Dad and Sheldon took us into an office with two computers. The monitors were huge, much bigger than the one we have at home. Images flashed on the screens. I recognized them from the software titles I'd played there before.

"Are we checking out something new?" I asked.

"You sure are," Sheldon tapped the keyboard on one of the computers, and the screensaver disappeared.

"It's a spelling program," Dad said.

"Spelling?" Zack made a face. "Who needs spelling?"

"You do. Otherwise you'll spend the rest of your life in grade seven," Dad laughed.

"Hockey players don't need to know how to spell, right Mitch?" Zack retorted.

"I guess not." I shrugged. Personally, I don't mind spelling. It makes reading a whole lot easier.

"This program is going to make spelling as much fun as hockey," Dad said. Zack looked doubtful.

"You're going to love it. I promise." Dad was clearly excited about the new program. "It's got the best features of an action game with plenty of interactive stuff. Here, Mitch, start it up." Dad pulled out a chair for me. The screen was filled with spinning letters. Some of them exploded, while the rest rotated into position forming the word "Spellbinder." A wacky little tune played out of the computer's speakers. Suddenly, the sound stopped and a door appeared. The words, "Opin, Opent, Open, Owpen" were printed on the door.

"Just click on the correct spelling, Mitch, and the door will open." I clicked "open" and, sure enough, the door creaked open. A bug dressed as a waiter was standing on the other side. He held out a menu card that read, "jetfighter, race car, motorcycle, moped."

"Now what?' asked Zack, pulling up a chair next to me.

"Pick the vehicle you want to cruise in," Dad replied. "But I warn you, the faster the vehicle, the faster things happen in this program. I'm going to leave you two to work through it. Mitch knows the drill. See you later." With that, Dad and Sheldon left us alone.

"Here goes nothing," Zack said as he clicked on the word "jetfighter." The screen suddenly looked like the cockpit of a jet. Zack's jetfighter moved very fast, while other planes with words on the side came at it from every direction. Some of the words were spelled right, others weren't. The object of the game was to blow the planes with the misspelled words away.

"Hey, this is hard," Zack complained.

"Maybe you should have started with a moped," I laughed. "We skipped a step. First you set your level."

We worked our way through the program. Whenever you weren't certain about a word, you could stop and ask for the meaning. Some words had pictures and even video clips. If you collected enough points you could move onto another level where things were completely different. Sometimes you blasted words away, other times you collected them and used them like money to buy stuff and go on little educational side trips. It was okay. Not as good as *Super Safari*, but nothing is as good as that one.

I left Zack exploring the wonderful world of words to have a look around some of the developers' desks. Ali Panju usually had the best stuff in progress. He wasn't in that day, so I fired up his computer for a little exploration of my own. While I waited for the system to boot up, I wandered down the hall to the lunch room for a pop. Dad was in Sheldon's office, talking and laughing. I was about to walk in and say hi, when I heard Zack's name.

"So you really think Zack's got that much talent?" Sheldon said.

"Enough to deserve special handling," Dad answered. "I talked to Fred, the boy's dad, and he agrees, provided it doesn't interfere with his schoolwork. It's not easy to find the time, so we're reworking his practice program, and I'm giving him extra ice time. He's a shoe-in for hockey camp."

The chair creaked as Sheldon leaned back. "Makes me glad my kids aren't into sports. Takes up way too much time. And how's Mitch doing on the team? Still Steady Eddie?"

From outside the door I mouthed the words, "Steady Eddie." What was that supposed to mean? I almost missed my dad's reply. "That's him, all right. Nothing to — " the ringing phone stopped him. "I'll let you get that." As Dad strode out of the office, he nearly caught me lurking by the door. I darted back to Ali's workstation, my heart pounding.

Zack and I had been friends since we were born. In fact, we were born on the same day. I always thought we were pretty much the same. Sure, I've always been a little better in school, but in everything else, we've been exactly alike. Until now.

The more I thought about what Dad had said, the more I couldn't believe it. It sounded like Dad already knew Zack was going to hockey camp almost two months before the announcement. What about me? Didn't he think I was as good as Zack? I was his son, not Zack. He should have been giving me extra practice.

I wasn't really concentrating when I started opening folders on Ali's computer. I kept thinking about the secret deal with Zack's dad. Did Zack know about it? If he did, why didn't he tell me? Like a robot I just kept opening folders inside folders inside folders in the computer directory. One of them looked interesting. It had a skull and crossbones on it. When I clicked on it, nothing happened for a second. Then the folder popped open to reveal three files. One of them was a program called "Black Hole." Now that looked cool. I double-clicked it, and within seconds everything on the monitor started disappearing like water down a drain. At first I thought it was a screensaver, but when I moved the mouse nothing happened — except everything on the screen continued to disappear bit by bit. It looked creepy to me, so I rebooted to stop it. The screen froze and nothing happened. I kept trying, but the computer wouldn't restart. Suddenly the screen started spitting up characters and bits of images. They flashed by at an alarming rate, making my eyes go buggy.

I ran down the hall to Zack. "What's up, Mitch?" he said, still engrossed in his spelling bee.

"Man, am I in trouble!" I exclaimed. "I messed up Ali's computer. Dad's gonna kill me."

At that moment I heard my dad's voice demand, "What the —"

I looked at Zack, but he hadn't caught on to what was happening. You see, my dad and Sheldon don't like me to play with the other guys' computers when they're not there.

"Mitch?" Dad's voice reached us seconds before he did. I wished I could go somewhere and hide. "Mitch, were you playing on Ali's machine?" I couldn't very well lie to him, even though I wanted to.

"Yeah," I said lamely. I followed him back to Ali's work-station. "I was just going to get you." Sure I was. Sheldon was standing at the desk, where the computer was still barfing up bytes.

"What was the last thing you did?" Sheldon asked me.

"I opened something called 'Black Hole.'" Dad and Sheldon looked at each other and back at me.

"Sorry," I mumbled.

"Go back to the other room, Mitch," Dad said. "Shel, call Ali, while I assess the damage."

"Dad, I — "

He cut me off. "Just go back and play with Zack, okay?" I felt guilty, but at least I had evened the score. My dad was as mad at me as I was at him.

5

Benchwarming 101

Mitch, touch my stick," Zack waved his hockey stick in my face. I grabbed the business end in both hands, letting my energy flow into the stick. "Thanks, man. Today I'm going for four goals. I need the extra voodoo."

Dustin banged the locker-room door open, stumbling into the room behind his enormous hockey bag. "I heard that, Zack. You can make your four goals after my four goals. And I don't need Mitch to kiss my stick to do it," he announced. All the other kids laughed. But Dustin still brought his stick over for me to touch. I know it's a silly superstition, but we've been doing it for so long we're afraid to stop. It started years ago when we were in learn-to-play. One of us would touch the sticks when we had a winning streak going. When the streak broke, we'd switch. Over the years it turned out that our longest streaks happened when I touched the sticks. So now, it's just me, all the time.

Dad came in with my freshly sharpened skates. "Here you go, kid," he smiled as he handed them over. I took them, smiling back awkwardly. Ever since the software incident, we'd been tense around each other.

"We're first on tonight, so don't waste time, get out there and warm up," Dad ordered. An exodus started as kids gathered up their gear and headed for the ice. I stood by the door, sticks tapping my outstretched hand as my teammates walked through.

Pucks were everywhere on the ice, zipping end to end as both teams took advantage of the extra warm-up time. Our opponents that night were the Etobicoke Eagles. They give us as much trouble as the North York Rangers, but in a different way. They have an outrageously good goalie who robs us blind. I thought Zack and Dustin were dreaming when they claimed they could score four apiece against him.

I scooped a puck from the Eagles end, brazenly threading through their players. Most of them just stared at the unaccustomed sight of an opposing player taking the offensive before the game even started. I smiled and nodded to a few of the players I knew by name. One of their defencemen made a half-hearted attempt to block me as I made my way toward the goal crease. Slipping around him easily, I faked a shot on goal, catching the goalie's eye. Instead of firing, I hooked around behind the net. "Hiya, there," I said, all friendly. Their defence got into the game, setting up on the other side of the net. The rest of their team milled around aimlessly. Debating whether to take their man on, I elected to turn and attack from the side I'd come in on. Despite my quick manoeuvre, the Eagles goalie anticipated my move. Wow, he really *could* play goal! Undaunted, I moved out in front of the net, jostling with the defenceman for position and a clear shot. For a second the puck came loose. Their player stabbed at it, but I managed to get it back. With only a little tickle to reassert my control, I pulled back and let one rip into their man at the net. Miraculously, it snuck under his arm. I let out a whoop that made everybody turn and stare. "Nice one." The Eagles goalie nodded at me.

"Thanks," I said smiling. "Plenty more where that came from."

He laughed. "Don't bet on it."

A whistle blew, calling me back to our bench. The rest of my team was lined up on the ice. Dad and Assistant Coach

Minelli conferred, glancing at some notes on a clipboard. I skated up to Zack. "Did you see that?" I asked.

"Sure. You were brilliant!" he crowed. "Thanks for breaking his spirit."

"All right, then," Dad said to get our attention. "We'll be making some minor changes tonight to our line assignments. We all want to make this team the winningest team in the league, and your assistant coach and I think these changes will spread our resources more evenly." He paused for a second, but it was long enough to let us start mumbling among ourselves. "Quiet please! Rothenberg you move to the A-line with Andermann and Lee. Stevens take over at centre on the B-line. Levitt and Tesma switch lines also."

I couldn't believe my ears! In fact, I almost took off my helmet because I thought it was interfering with my hearing. The rest of the B-line started for the bench, while Zack looked at me pityingly.

"What gives?" I said.

"Beats me, Mitch. Why don't you go ask your dad?"

Dad was about ten feet away, so I started moving in his direction, when Johnny Wolsky cruised by.

"Buzzzzzz," he murmured in passing.

"What's that, Wolsky?" I snarled. "You got something to say to me?" I got his meaning all right. I was a "B"-liner. He kept right on buzzing. I took a run at him, knocking him down on the ice. Johnny scrambled to his feet and tore after me. Grabbing each other's sweaters, we struggled until Dad came over to pull us apart.

"What's going on here?" he bellowed.

I was so angry I bellowed right back at him. "I don't know. *You* tell me what's going on!" I threw my stick on the ice in disgust. Wolsky, in the meantime, was still buzzing faintly. I lunged at him, but Dad had me in a deathgrip. "Let me go!" I yelled, feeling my voice rise in frustration. Dad loosened his grip for a moment, long enough for me to dart away and pick up my stick. I angrily whacked the boards a couple of times. The rest of the team had stopped what they were doing and were staring at my outburst.

"Mitch, get off the ice. You're holding up the game." Dad pointed in the direction of the bench.

The ref was talking a mile a minute, but I couldn't hear him. I whacked the boards again.

"MITCHELL STEVENS! GET OFF THE ICE!" Dad's voice boomed in the vast arena. Everybody in the building was looking at me. I skated with as much dignity as I could gather to the bench, kicking my way to the last seat in the row.

Finally, mercifully, the game started. Seconds later Wolsky went off-side, halting play. As he passed the bench, he began buzzing, just loud enough for me to hear. Leaping to my feet, I swung my stick in front of him, and almost sent him sprawling to the ice again. Dad jumped nearly four feet into the air, whirling around to fix me with an angry glare. "That's it, Mitch. You sit out this period. Fraser, you're on for Stevens."

"Dad!"

"No discussion, Mitchell," he said, his face bright red. "Whatever bee you've got in your bonnet, clear it out fast."

***

By the time I got in the game, Zack already had two goals, and it looked like the new A-line was getting along okay without me. I was still pretty steamed, but I'd also been itching to get onto the ice and make something happen for the lowly B-line, which hadn't scored a goal yet. When Dad whistled me onto the ice I felt a rush of excitement. Mad or not, I was getting at least two goals of my own!

Natalie Plaxton and James Friesen were my wingers. Smiling and spouting inspirational slogans, they seemed pleased to have me on their line. I took my place for the face off. The Eagles centre was someone I'd never tangled with before, but he looked a bit dopey to me. The ref bounced the puck between us and, *whoosh*, that kid's stick was on it. It took a second for me to react to my mistake, and taking advantage of some bobbling by their right wing, I managed to reclaim the puck.

Glancing up for my wingers, I discovered Natalie and James, their eyes riveted on me, looking eager as beavers for the pass. A good start, I thought. I was closer to James, but Natalie was in a better position to take the puck up the ice. I fired her a shot, praying she would be able to control it, if she snared it at all. Beaming, Natalie handled the puck with some difficulty across the blue line just ahead of me. A swarm of Eagles surrounded her. Just as she lifted her stick to fire it back to me while I muscled in on the goal, an Eagle scooped it. Natalie's face fell seconds before she did. "Get up, Nat!" I shouted as I reversed direction to chase the puck, which was being carried back into our end.

No way was I going to end this shift without a goal. James actually made it to the other end first. He flew into the boards after the puck, joining an Eagle player, digging for rubber. The Eagle player flipped a wobbly that landed within the reach of James's stick. He poked it away from another incoming Eagle, giving me just enough time to catch up with it. This time I'd already scoped for a target, and with Natalie at the point I had to trust that she'd hold the pass long enough for me to set up at the net. The backhand went smoothly across the ice to land with a nice solid smack against Nat's stick. For once she kept her head up, keeping me in her sights and the puck on her stick as she slid sideways to clear the pesky Eagle defence.

"Now!" I screamed, and Nat instinctively whacked a pass that very nearly cleared me, the net, the building and possibly the tennis courts next door. You can't jump very well on skates, but somehow I managed to knock the puck down. Unfortunately, I knocked it right in front of the Eagle centre, who I now saw had a wicked gleam in his eye. We fought for the puck, but this one was mine. The Eagles goalie homed on the play like radar. The second I saw him lean to my right I fired one between his knee and his elbow. He almost got a piece of it, but in the end I got my goal and a roar of approval from my exultant linemates.

Between shifts, Nat and James were absolutely bubbling with glee. And for a guy who just got demoted, Mark Levitt, who used to be on the A-line with me, even seemed pleased.

"Good work, all of you," my dad said as we piled onto the bench. "Nice going, Mitch."

For a second I forgot that he was the enemy and simply said, "Thanks."

At that point the score was three to two, for us. Seconds before our next shift, Zack drew a penalty for roughing. One minute and forty-three seconds of our shift we would have to play short-handed. That didn't give me much of a chance to score another goal. The A-line skated to the bench at the change, and Dad waved Johnny Wolsky back onto the ice, holding Natalie back. I could see the disappointment on her face, but I knew we needed the extra defenceman. "Welcome to the B-line, Wolsky," I jeered.

That minute–forty-three seemed like an eternity, with Levitt, Friesen and Wolsky body-blocking the Eagle attack. Whenever they could come up with the puck, they'd fire it for me to take into Eagle territory. Hanging back at the blue line, I spied the opportunity I was waiting for. Every Eagle on the ice was within three metres of our net, peppering Matt with shots he deflected admirably. Seizing the moment, I shouted

for James Friesen, who had just scooped the loose puck away
from the net. He froze, looking around frantically in the direction of my voice. His slight hesitation almost lost him the
puck, but when he finally sighted me his stick connected for
one of the best passing shots of his pee wee hockey career.
Wolsky, positioned between James and me, immediately
skated to my left. Together we fled for the blue line, with me
crossing just in front of Wolsky. I angled in on the goal while
five Eagles tore up the ice behind me. Now it was just their
goalie and me. He waited for me to signal my shot with a
move, a twitch or a nod. What the heck, I thought, here goes
nothing. Slapshot! Never letting up speed I chased it down,
ready for the rebound if it came. Instead the puck carried right
past his left shoulder into the net. Goal! James jumped on my
back, babbling incoherently about his assist. Even Johnny
Wolsky gave me a big slap on the back.

As it turned out, my goal was the game winner. We had a
five-to-two victory, with Dustin scoring the last goal. But the
talk in the dressing room was all about the B-line's short-
handed goal. Zack sat down beside me to undress. "You did
okay on the B-line," he said without looking at me.

"Is that supposed to make it all right?" I retorted. "That
I'm the new star of the B-line?" Suddenly I was angry again.
"Why didn't you stick up for me?" I asked him.

"What do you mean? I'm not the coach, I don't make the
rules," he said, frowning stubbornly. "It's got nothin' to do
with me."

"That's bull and you know it. Friends stick up for each
other," I persisted.

Zack's face was getting red. "Yeah, and get benched for a
whole period."

"Forget it!" I said, stomping angrily into the hall. I stood
there shaking my head. Like everybody else, Zack just didn't
get it.

6

Knock-out at the Gardens

My birthday was coming up on February 23 and I wondered if my folks were cooking up something with Zack's parents. Zack and I had celebrated every birthday together for years. When we were little kids our parents would plan these big joint parties, but as we got older they let us decide how we wanted to celebrate. The way I was feeling about Zack I couldn't get in the mood to plan something. I figured I'd wait and see if things improved.

Until that winter, I would have said that nothing on earth could have come between us. I guess it shows how wrong you can be. Since the last game Zack and I had been kind of tense around each other. In fact, things were kind of tense all around. And with my dad waltzing around like Mr. NHL Coach, all happy and proud of how his team was doing, it was a bit much to take. A couple of times I considered talking to him about what was bothering me, but you'd be amazed at how difficult it is to find the right moment, even when someone's right there beside you.

"Doing anything tonight, Mitch?" Mom asked.

"Nah. Just going to hang around here and clean my room," I replied, smirking at the likelihood of spending my birthday cleaning my room.

"Maybe you could go with Dad to pick up the new laundry tub," she said.

Oh sure, like we're really going to the hardware store. Mom's "surprises" are always so obvious, but I play along to make her happy. I went to find Dad. "Mom says you're going to get the laundry tub tonight."

"No," he replied, "I brought some work home. We'll go tomorrow." Now I really was surprised.

It's not like nobody wished me happy birthday all day. Mom, Dad and Jennifer all made a big deal at breakfast. And then they forgot all about it.

We ate dinner earlier than usual, and just as Jen and I were clearing the plates before dessert, the phone rang. Dad jumped up to answer, but instead of going to the phone in the kitchen he took it in the den. Within seconds he was back. "Get your coat, Mitch. We're going out. Now."

Without waiting for my reply, he dashed from the room, grabbed his coat and was out the door. I followed him to the van.

"Where are we going?" I said. "Or should I ask?"

"You can ask," he replied. "But I'm not saying."

We drove in silence for a while. It looked like we were going to Dad's office. We headed along Davenport, following it across Yonge where it becomes Church Street. Dad hummed to the music on the radio. South of Wellesley he started swivelling his head around like a turtle. Finally he wheeled the van into a parking lot.

"Hop out, Bucko," he said cheerfully. "We're here." I hopped out, following him down Church Street. The Gardens loomed before us. A lightbulb went on in my head. We were going to a Leafs game.

Just inside the front doors Zack and Mr. Andermann stood waiting for us. I greeted Zack awkwardly, still feeling uncomfortable after our angry words. Before we took our seats, our dads stopped by a booth that sold souvenirs and bought sweaters. They put our names and numbers on them.

Our seats were in the Gold section. We'd never sat there before and it was awesome — so close to the ice you could almost touch the players. That night the Leafs were playing Colorado, and since it was their first year as the Avalanche instead of the Quebec Nordiques, nobody expected much. "Piece of cake," Zack announced. "The Leafs will bury them."

"I wouldn't be too certain, son," Mr. Andermann interjected.

And sure enough Colorado blew our Leafs away. As things went from bad to worse for the Leafs, Zack and I got more and more bummed out. I really hated the idea that they would lose on my birthday. It was just one more thing to go wrong.

I sat on the aisle so I wouldn't bother anyone by getting up for food and stuff, and Zack sat next to me. We weren't saying much to each other, and after awhile I noticed that he was talking a lot to my Dad. Actually, Dad and Zack were having a great time analyzing the plays and joking around. "Hey, it's my birthday too!" I thought. "What's the deal?" Leaning across Zack, I tried to get in on the conversation. They were laughing like hyenas. "What's so funny?" I asked.

"Nothing," Zack said sharply.

I looked at Dad, but his attention was back on the game.

"What are you guys talking about?" I wasn't about to give it up.

"Coach was just talking about stickhandling," Zack replied dismissively.

I figured the best way to stickhandle the situation was to change places with Zack. If anybody was going to get advice from my dad, it was going to be me. "I want to switch seats for a while," I stated.

And then out of nowhere Zack said the dumbest thing.

"They're playing like a bunch of B-line bozos," he exclaimed in disgust.

"What? What did you call them?" I jumped to the defence of B-liners everywhere.

Zack looked at me strangely. "I said they were playing like B-liners."

"And what's wrong with B-liners, eh?" I could feel the blood flooding my face.

"What's your problem, Mitch?" he said.

"So you think you could save this game, Mr. Sure Shot?" I retorted, still stinging from his comment.

"Yeah, I could. At least I'm not on the B-team!" That was the last straw. I leaped to my feet, grabbing Zack by the front of his brand-new Leaf's jersey. With a surprised look, Zack stood to face me, trying to peel my hands off his sweater. "Chill out, man," he said.

"I am chilled!" I exclaimed, spinning him around. He struggled to free himself from my grasp. Out of the corner of my eye I could see my dad and Mr. Andermann get out of their seats. I shoved Zack hard. His back was to the seats in front of us and he lost his balance, toppling over onto two men in the row below. Zack came up swinging, trying to climb over the men.

"Hey you, get those kids out of here!" a big guy in a baseball cap shouted at my dad. The big guy and his bigger friend dumped Zack into the aisle. Dad hesitated for a moment as if he were going to say something, then decided not to. In the meantime, I dove on Zack and we flailed at each other, bumping down the steps with our dads running to catch up.

Lashing out wildly, some of our shots connected. Zack got me a few times around the chest and shoulder, while I managed to land one under Zack's eye. Still punching, our dads hauled us apart. Zack's jersey was ripped and we were both covered with garbage.

By that time, nobody in our section was watching the game any more. Some people were really annoyed, while others egged us on.

"What is going on here!?" my dad demanded.

I looked at Zack angrily before I answered. "Nothing. Nothing's going on. Forget it."

"Zack?" Mr. Andermann addressed his son. Zack just stood there glaring right back at me. Dad pulled me into a seat, apologizing to the people around us for the disturbance.

"This isn't over, Mitch," Dad said. "You can't behave like this and dismiss it as nothing. We are definitely going to have a talk when we get home."

With our fathers between us, Zack and I quietly fumed for the rest of the game as the Leafs sank under the weight of the Avalanche.

7

Dad Drones On

The trip home from the Gardens was pretty tense with Dad giving me sideways looks. We drove the entire way in silence. I went straight to my room as soon as I got in the house. I turned my stereo on and set the volume really low so I wouldn't give my parents an excuse to come up and bug me some more. I tried to relax, but seeing the trophies and team pictures that decorated my room made me angry all over again. There we were, Zack and I, mugging for the camera, front and centre. On the wall next to my Leafs poster was a glossy picture of the Muskoka hockey camp, with "You are here" written in black marker and a little picture of me stuck to it. Mom had put it there. "Yeah, sure," I said out loud. Taking a marker out of my desk, I crossed out "here" and wrote "nowhere." "Yep, that's me, Nowhere Man." Like I had the slightest chance to make it there now.

A sharp knock on the door made me jump. Before I could answer, Dad was in the room. Closing the door behind him, he went over to the bed and sat down. "Uh-oh," I thought, "here it comes."

"What's going on, Mitch?" he said, not wasting any time.

"Nothing. Just getting ready for bed, you know," I replied, deflecting his question.

He tried another approach. "Pretty disappointing game tonight, eh?"

"Yeah." I wasn't giving him much to work with.

"Your mom taped it so we could watch later and see if we were on TV."

"That's cool."

"Maybe they caught the fight." Now he was taunting me.

"Yeah, maybe I should try wrestling or boxing instead of hockey," I shot back.

Seeing the confused look on my dad's face only increased my frustration. Ever since he became coach it seemed like he'd changed. I was never sure who I was talking to — Dad or Coach Stevens. Back in the good old days, I could talk to Dad about stuff that happened at hockey or school and he'd help me work it out. Now we didn't talk about me any more. It was always the team. I was sick of the team.

"Mitch, I know there's something wrong. You've never been in fights before. You know that fighting is unacceptable. I need to know why you're doing it."

Well, I needed to know why he was doing what he was doing to me. Sticking your own kid on the B-line when he was clearly A-line material was not exactly acceptable either. And I told him so.

"What's this got to do with Zack?" he asked.

Boy, he just didn't get it. Here I was pouring my heart out and he missed the point entirely.

"Zack, Zack, Zack, Zack," I whined, "that's all I ever hear any more. Forget Zack. I'm talking about me!" My voice was rising and I could hear the blood pounding in my brain.

"Okay, Mitch," he said quietly, "let's talk about you."

"You heard what I said, didn't you?" I replied.

"I heard it all," he said.

"So?" I waited for his words of wisdom. Instead he just looked more baffled than ever.

"About the B-team, Dad." I was getting exasperated. My father was talking about fighting and Zack. I was talking about me, Muskoka and the drones. Some conversation.

"I'll tell you what, Mitch," Dad finally answered. "I'm going to go downstairs and get us both some birthday cake. When I come back in, we'll start over. Okay?"

I nodded. At least it would give me time to think about how I could make my feelings clear to him. As far as I was concerned, my dad wasn't leaving the room again without promising to put me back on the A-line.

He was back a few minutes later with two huge pieces of chocolate cake and a couple of glasses of cold milk. We ate our cake in silence.

"Nobody bakes a cake like your mother," he exclaimed proudly.

There was a long pause, with neither of us wanting to start again.

"Go ahead, Mitch," he said at last. "You have my undivided attention." He reached over to turn off the stereo. The sudden silence made me instantly uncomfortable. Dad looked at me expectantly.

"Um, like I was saying," I started, pausing to gather my thoughts.

"As you were saying," he repeated.

Oh good, I thought, a grammar lesson. Just what I need. With that thought all the rest went out of my head and for a moment I was completely lost. I struggled to get my mind back on track.

Dad cleared his throat. "Sorry," he said. "I interrupted you. Go on."

"Ever since you demoted me to B-line, Zack's been acting like a jerk." That pretty much covered it as far as I was concerned.

"You weren't demoted, Mitch. And Zack hasn't been acting differently. In fact, you're the one who's acting up."

"If I wasn't demoted, why am I still on the B-line? Why have I been on the B-line at all?" I whined.

Sighing, Dad gave me a long, weary look. "I made some line changes to benefit the whole team. As far as I'm concerned there is no A or B-line, there are just two equally important lines, and right now they're both working."

"Ha, ha, ha," I snorted. "All you ever do is work with the A-line. Assistant Coach Minelli works with us. Second-string coach, second-string line."

"Now, Mitch," Dad said calmly, "you know that's not true. We have completely balanced practices."

"Why me? Why not Zack on the B-line?" I was just warming up. "Why not Dustin or — "

"Because you were the right person for the job," he interrupted again.

"Are you sure I just wasn't the only kid whose Dad wouldn't pitch a fit if you demoted him?"

Dad's face got really red. I knew I'd put my foot in it, but I was on a downhill slide and nothing was stopping me.

"Before you were coach, we used to joke about the B-line. Remember, we'd laugh at some of the dumb plays they made?" I had him there. It was true, a few times we'd had a good chuckle over some of the stupid moves that Natalie and James made.

It was a long time before he spoke. "Yes, that's true," he said finally. "And may I remind you, we also laughed at the dumb plays you and the A-line made too."

Okay, we were even. Even Stevens. But it was no joke as far as I was concerned.

"You're ruining my chances of getting to hockey camp and playing on the select team!" I blurted. "I'm stuck playing with the drones and fighting for every measly point, while Zack gets all the goals and the glory. It's not fair."

"Please stop calling your teammates drones, Mitch." My father's voice had an angry edge now.

"Why? Everybody calls them drones. I bet you called your B-line drones way back when you were in Pee Wee, too," I challenged.

"They're valuable to the team, Mitch. Everyone contributes, James, Natalie — "

I broke in, "Oh yeah, Natalie. She's a regular Queen Bee."

"That's enough, Mitch." Dad stood up and headed to the door. "We'll continue this when you've cooled down."

I made one final desperate appeal. "It's just not fair. You're the coach, it's your job — "

Dad's voice coldly cut me off. "Yes, I am the coach, and maybe it looks to you like putting you with Natalie and James's line isn't fair. My job isn't to be fair to *you*; my job is to do what's right and fair for the whole team." He strode out of the room without a backward glance.

8

Knock-out, Round Two

It had been three weeks since my demotion to the B-line. Even though we were winning games, I still felt wasted in the B-line boonies. Not to mention the fact that we only had a month to go in the season and my chances of winning a spot at the special hockey camp were about zip. Meanwhile, Zack continued to tear up the ice, flicking goals around and generally looking like a star. It was true that the B-line had boosted production since I joined them, and Natalie and James were skating better, taking some chances and playing with more confidence. But it was still the boonies. And being leader of the drones was not exactly my goal in life.

"Check your gear, Mitch," Dad said as we prepared to leave for the arena. "You wouldn't want to forget something and jinx our streak."

"I've got everything," I replied confidently. Tonight's game was critical for us. The Stingers were currently enjoying the top spot with a one-point lead over the Rangers. A win would put us up three points. Not much, but a loss would put us behind.

"Any line changes tonight, Dad?" I ventured hesitantly.

"I don't think so, Mitch. Things are going pretty well the way they are." Dad didn't take the bait. I really wanted to ask him again if I could go back to the A-line, but I couldn't quite bring myself to do it since our argument.

For some reason we arrived at the arena later than usual that evening. The dressing room was already crowded with kids, parents and mounds of equipment. While Dad went off for his pre-game pow-wow with Assistant Coach Minelli, I prepared my gear.

Natalie stood fidgeting nearby, all dressed and ready to go. "I am so nervous," she said, plunking herself down on the bench beside me.

"Take it easy, Nat," I replied. "You're playing fine."

"Do you think so?" She seemed doubtful, but smiled behind her face guard. Then she got all serious again. "I haven't scored a goal all season. You can't get any respect on this team if you don't score goals."

"That's not true," I retorted, even though I knew it was. "We're a team. We work together." Now I was sounding like my dad.

"It's easy for you to say that, Mitch. You score goals all the time. But if you weren't on the B-line with us, we wouldn't even be talking right now. You'd be sitting with Zack, looking at us like we were bugs or something."

It was pretty hard to argue with the truth. I could feel my face redden a bit as I struggled to find the right thing to say. We both knew that what she said was true. "Not any more, Nat," I finally mumbled.

At that moment, Zack came in and, ignoring me, sat down on the opposite side of the room. No big deal. I never acted like a megastar when I was on the A-line. I guess all the attention was going to his swelled head.

I watched him pull his helmet out of his bag. "Better check to see if it still fits," I taunted.

"Sure it does," Zack shot back. "It's size A."

Score even. I continued to check my equipment. Skates, gloves, helmet, stick — they were all there, just like I told my dad. And I put everything on in the order the team had decided on. It's a team superstition that during a winning streak, nobody washes their sweater, their socks, their jocks, anything. And everything we did had to follow the right order — from putting on our equipment to who leaves the locker room first. Everything was fine until I got to the jersey part of the program. I looked into my bag in disbelief. It wasn't there. "Dusty, can you go get my dad?" I asked, seeing that my friend was already dressed.

"I can't, Mitch. We haven't finished the ritual. Send Cam."

I looked around for Dustin's little brother.

"Cam, I need you to go get my dad, the coach, right away." The kid ran out of the dressing room, and I hoped he had some idea where he was going.

He reappeared moments later with my dad. "What's the problem?" Dad looked concerned.

"My sweater's not in my bag."

"Didn't I tell you to check before we left?" he replied, clearly exasperated. I felt about two inches tall in front of the team.

"Dad," I pleaded, "can we talk about that later? Right now I need my jersey."

He strode off, presumably looking for a phone.

Fortunately our house was only five minutes away from St. Mike's arena. With any luck my mom or my sister would be home. I waited as patiently as I could, considering the rest of the team was shooting me looks that would melt ice. They couldn't finish the pre-game ritual without me. And we had only seven minutes to go until game time. I didn't like the smirk on Zack's face, but I wasn't exactly in a position to do anything about it.

Two minutes before game time, Dad came running in with a spare jersey from the car. "Put this on. We can't wait," he ordered.

"But isn't Mom coming?" I wailed.

"You can change on the bench when she gets here." The grumbling started immediately. The rest of the team quickly realized that our ritual was about to be destroyed. And with it our luck.

At that moment the door burst open, and Mom flew in, nearly tripping over two kids and a bag. She waved my sweater aloft and sent it spinning over heads right into my arms. Relieved, I struggled into it. With the sweater still over my head, I heard her words as if I was under water. "It was still in the dryer."

The team gasped in unison.

My head popped out. "You *washed* it?"

Mom was beaming innocently. "Of course. It stunk."

I looked around at fourteen dejected faces. "No Mom, *this* stinks."

***

I wish I could say it didn't matter. But the team was so bummed out they wouldn't even let me touch their sticks. Maybe they should have.

The very first shift, the Rangers top scorer caught Matt napping in goal and slapped one by. Everyone looked down the bench at me, including the guys on the ice. Even Matt seemed to blame me, although with his goalie's mask it was hard to tell.

Twenty minutes into the game we were down three–zip. Dad was tearing his remaining hair out. The only consolation for me was that I didn't have to face old MORG. But she passed me coming off the ice and gave me an evil sneer. I got shivers.

With no production out of either line, it was looking hopeless. I decided the only way to get back in favour with the team would be to win the game single-handed. And believe me, that's how it seemed out there. I felt like a stray cat at a dog convention. We were in their end and still down by three, when I caught a toss and banked it off the boards behind a Rangers defenceman. Natalie got to the puck first and made a good pass to James. James did his best, but he was no match for the Ranger who promptly stole the puck. I raced after the Ranger player who struggled to control the puck at centre ice. I had my stick out just as he tapped it forward toward his linemate. I was able to deflect the puck enough to deny the Ranger another shot at it.

The puck was mine again. Natalie was in good position at the net with James on the point. I had a clear shot at James and he held on to the puck until he could make a solid pass to Natalie. The puck hit Natalie's stick about the same time she was hit from behind by a Ranger. She fell forward onto the ice and valiantly tried to scoop the puck around into the goal. Instead she only succeeded in handing it over to a Ranger who broke for our end while we struggled to regroup.

I'd made the mistake of losing track of my linemates' locations on the ice and before I realized that we were all clumped in enemy territory, a Ranger was rushing in on our undefended goal. I didn't even make it to centre ice by the time his stick arced up for a slapshot. Matt never had a chance. The puck rocketed under his outstretched leg.

Natalie skated up with a woeful look. We cruised to the bench together. As we got close we could hear some grumbling from our teammates. "Nice play, Natalie," Zack jeered with obvious sarcasm.

"Hey, leave her alone!" I shouted at him. Nat was just doing what she'd seen Zack and me do successfully in the past. "You've tried that move a million times, Zack. You're just lucky it never backfired on *you!*" I stopped myself from saying it was simply bad luck, in case he jumped all over me for jinxing the team. He had no idea that the Bs worked as hard or harder than the A-line.

"I can defend myself, Mitch," Natalie said, her face turning red. I expected her to tell Zack to back off, but she just glared at him and sat down.

Dad stopped me before I got on the bench. "Mitch," he said, "you stay on for this shift." Overjoyed, I flew back to the face-off circle to take my old place on the A-team. I wasn't even bothered by MORG, who seemed to find newer and uglier ways to glare at me.

"Try to stay on your feet," I said, baiting her. She merely scowled some more. "Witty comeback," I continued. Our little chat ended as the ref dropped the puck between us.

She got the puck and the last laugh as her stick wedged between my skates, flipping me onto my back like a flopping fish. Without a word she skated away to join the play. Before I got back onto my feet, the Rangers had another goal.

Zack zoomed over, pulling me up roughly. "What do you think you're doing?" he shouted in frustration. "You might as well have put that goal in our net yourself."

He skated off, with me in hot pursuit.

"What's your problem?" I yelled at his back. "Mr. Pointless!"

He whirled around, skating into my face. "Buzz off, Mitch," he snarled. "Yeah, buzz off back to the B-line."

My gloves were off before I even thought about hitting him. I lashed out at him, driving him to the ice in an effort to rip his helmet off. He flailed at me, but I had him pinned with my knees on his shoulders. If the Puck Police hadn't pulled me off, I might have done something I'd really regret. Whistles were blowing everywhere. Over the pounding of my heart, I could hear my dad shouting my name.

The ref skated over to Dad at the bench, while the linesman skated me away from Zack toward the penalty box. "Hey!" I yelled at him. "Where are we going?"

"Penalty," he replied.

"How can you give a penalty for two guys fighting on the same team?"

He hesitated, looking over at the ref, who was talking heatedly with my dad. Finally the ref skated away and my dad waved me over. Zack was already on the far end of the bench.

With his face like a big purple grape just inches from mine, Dad sputtered through clenched teeth, "You're both out of the game."

"It's not like I killed anybody," I mumbled.

"Sit down, or go to the dressing room!" Dad shouted. "You're very lucky you didn't get a suspension." With that, he strode off.

Sitting out the rest of the game wasn't any worse than being in it. The Rangers toasted us six to nothing.

9

No Exit

The dressing room was deadly quiet after the game. Even the parents picked up on our mood of doom. Zack and I sat in opposite corners, avoiding each other's eyes. Our moms shot us worried looks as they chatted in low voices by the door. When the Andermanns filed out of the dressing room, Mom came over to sit beside me.

"Mitch? What happened out there?" she asked.

"I don't want to talk about it, okay?" I answered. I was trying to be honest.

"Is it about the sweater?"

"No, Mom. Can we just drop it, please?"

Her face looked sad, but she dropped the subject. "I'm going to the grocery store. Is there anything you want me to pick up?" she announced.

"Nah," I mumbled in reply.

With that she stood and headed for the door, giving me one last worried glance as she departed. I gathered up my things, heading out by myself. Probably the last thing I wanted to do was drive home with my dad.

Outside in the parking lot, four Rangers players, MORG included, were whooping it up, chanting, "We're number one! We're number one!" It was more than I could bear. I flung the van's hatch up furiously. Dad came running toward the van shouting, "Mitch! Be careful!" Dumping my gear into the back,

I very carefully inched the van door back down, taking about two minutes to close it. "Was that careful enough, Dad?"

Without answering, he slid into the van and put the key into the ignition. I hopped onto the passenger seat, reaching for my seatbelt. Instead of starting the car, Dad turned to me. His face looked stern in the dim light. "What's going on, Mitch?"

"Nothing." I folded my arms across my chest, staring straight ahead.

"We're not going anywhere until I get some answers," Dad said.

Snapping off my seatbelt, I reached for the door handle. I was foiled when Dad snapped the automatic locks shut.

"Mitch, stop it!" he said, his voice rising in anger. I popped the lock up on my side, only to have him pop it back down. For what seemed like an hour the only sound in the car was the clunk, snap, clunk of the locks going up and down.

Finally, in utter frustration, I blurted it all out. "You're screwing up my chance to go to the hockey camp because you think Zack's better than me!" Dad recoiled as my words hit him in the face. "You've already voted for Zack to join the select team. And you don't even care if your own son works like a dog on the second-string. You're a lousy dad and a lousier coach!"

Dad turned to me, a shocked look on his face. "Mitch, do you really think that as the coach I should only be concerned with what you want?"

"No," I spat back, "but you should at least care about me!" Before he had a chance to respond, I popped the lock once more, and half expecting Dad to slam it back down again, I threw myself against the door. Instead, it opened, and I spilled out into the parking lot. I tried to scramble over the snowbank, but my feet skidded out from under me and I slid, head first, under the van. I heard a door open and I could see my father's legs run around to my side.

"Get me out of here!" I pleaded. My head was wedged beside the wheel, and my mouth was full of snow and sand.

Dad's hands grasped my ankles. "Watch your head, Mitch," he said as he gently pulled me up the slope of the snowbank. I was hanging there upside down when he began to chuckle. "It's a good thing for the team that you're better on skates than you are on your feet." And for the first time since Dad became coach, we had a good laugh.

We got back in the car, but Dad still didn't start it. For a second I thought he was going to begin lecturing me again. Instead he said, "Do you really think I'm a lousy dad?" Seeing the hurt look on his face, I rushed to reassure him. "No, of course not."

"But I'm still a lousy coach, right?"

My indignation returned momentarily, but I stopped myself from agreeing with him.

"Would you like to know why I did what I did?" he asked.
I nodded.

Dad sat thinking for a minute, like he wasn't sure how to begin. "Maybe I can explain it like this," he said finally. "I'd have to say you and Zack are equally good players, Mitch. But you have very different styles. Zack's talent is in his power and speed. He scores a lot of goals and gets the glory because of it. You're different. Your talent is in making things happen. You're a playmaker. And a lot of those plays wind up as goals scored by Zack. Do you see what I mean?" He looked at me and I could tell how much he wanted me to understand.

"I guess so," was all I could think to say.

He continued, "I moved you onto the other line so the whole team could benefit from your skill. You don't realize how much the team looks to you for leadership. And look what happened. Suddenly the B-line, which rarely scored all season, was racking up points right alongside the A-line.

Morale went up, we shot to the top of the league. And all that because of a simple change — moving some players around."

I thought about that for a minute. "So why didn't you just tell me all that before you moved me?" I wasn't going to let him off the hook just yet.

"Hey, it's not easy being Coach Dad. For one thing, I didn't want your head to swell up like a balloon — which it may be doing right now," he replied.

I deflated a little.

"Everyone, A-line and B-line, boys and girls, has a job to do on the team. I can't have kids thinking they're hot stuff because they're on the A-line and everyone else is useless. My job is to help everyone play the best they can. Together."

I knew that what Dad said was true. I'd had the opportunity to see for myself how hard my B-line teammates worked. I guess my attitude toward them *had* changed. In the past I had never had much respect for them. I was beginning to see how depressing it must be to play on a team with a bunch of guys who treated you like you were second-rate. I was also beginning to feel a bit ashamed of myself.

Dad started the car. "I'm sorry, Mitch. I hope you can forgive me. I made a mistake in not explaining it to you. Look how it backfired."

Oh yeah, that. I'd almost forgotten about the blow-up between Zack and me. Dad stuck out his hand and I shook it solemnly. We rode home silently, deep in our own private thoughts.

Mr. Andermann's truck was parked in front of our house when we got there. I was suddenly very excited. I was sure that if I told Zack everything Dad had told me, we could straighten things out between us. Without collecting my bag from the back of our van, I ran into the house. Mr. Andermann was in the kitchen drinking coffee with Mom. "Where's Zack?" I asked.

"Hi, Mitch. He's not with me," Mr. Andermann replied.

"Oh."

When Dad came in, Mom called to him. "Joe, Fred's here. We're in the kitchen." Dad shrugged his coat off, leaving it over the post at the foot of the stairs. The two men greeted each other like they hadn't set eyes on one another in years. It was kind of odd, considering they'd parted company only an hour before. Dad reached into the cupboard for a mug. He waved the coffee pot at Mom and Mr. Andermann.

"Refills?" he inquired. They shook their heads. Dad filled his mug and then led Mr. Andermann into the family room.

Not being invited in, I left Mom in the kitchen and lurked out of sight around the corner, where I could hear them just fine.

"Tough game today, Joe. Sometimes I think those kids put too much store in these superstitions," Mr. Andermann said.

"I had a talk with Mitch on the way home. I think we got to the bottom of the problem," I heard Dad say.

"Actually, Zack and I had a talk ourselves," Mr. Andermann replied. There was a long pause. "Zack wants a trade."

"What?" Dad echoed my thoughts.

"It's what he wants," Mr. Andermann continued. "I think it's wrong, especially this late in the season, but we have to keep him motivated to play well. Right now he's got it in his head that the Stingers are going down the tube."

Without thinking, I burst into the room. "Let me talk to him," I pleaded. "I can make him change his mind. Please!"

Both men looked at me. Finally Mr. Andermann said, "It would be great if you could, but I warn you, Mitch, if he says no, I'm not going to force him. Agreed?"

Confidently I nodded my consent. "Can we go right now?"

I waited impatiently for them to finish their coffee. Finally, Dad and I got back in the van and followed Mr. Andermann to Zack's house.

Zack was in his room when we got there, playing music really loud. I knocked a couple of times, but he didn't hear me. At least he didn't answer the door. I opened it cautiously in case he fired something at me when he saw who it was. He was on his bed reading a comic book.

"Yo, Zack," I said tentatively.

"Buzz off, Bee Boy," he replied snarkily.

I let it pass, pulling up the chair from his desk.

"I guess you didn't hear me with all that buzzing in your ears."

Taking a deep breath I launched into the little speech I had prepared. "Listen, Zack, it was all a big misunderstanding, and now that Dad's explained it to me, I realize how important I am to the team, and we shouldn't be fighting." I paused to collect my thoughts.

Zack threw the comic down on the bed and stood up to face me. For a second I felt a little intimidated. "How important *you* are? That's rich, man. If you're so important what are you doing in the Bs?"

Realizing that my words had come out wrong, I tried again. "I mean we're all important, and since I've been on the B-line the whole team's been better."

"Yeah, we're so much better we're losing. We've gone from Stingers to Losers in one game." Zack was glaring at me defiantly.

I needed to get the conversation back on track. "I hear you're talking trade," I replied.

"So what?" he answered. "I gotta think about my future."

"Your future? Get a grip, Zack. You're only thirteen!"

"I can't concentrate on my game with maniacs like you sabotaging me," he shot back.

"One game more and we're back on top," I cried. Zack's stubbornness was making it difficult to get my point across.

"Do it without me. I can't trust you. And I'm going to Muskoka one way or the other," Zack said. Returning to his comic, he growled, "Get out."

10

Gone but Not Forgotten

Zack went off to the North Toronto Hurricanes amid rumours and speculation. My teammates on the Stingers were more than a little unhappy with me. Zack's replacement, Erik Swanson, had a reputation for being trouble on a team. Dad wasn't too happy about that, but Erik also had some impressive stats. At our first practice without Zack, Dad asked me if I wanted back on the A-line. I jumped at the chance.

When they heard, Natalie and James looked at me as if I'd set them adrift in the ocean on a matchstick. "Come on, guys," I pleaded. "And Nat. You'll do great without me. Really." They looked sceptical.

"They don't need you on the A-line," said Natalie, flicking her braid at me like a long red finger.

"Yeah," James interjected. "They have plenty of fire power."

"And we play better with you at centre." Nat looked around sheepishly. "I don't want Ian Rothenberg to hear me say that. He'd be ticked."

"Ian's playing a lot better now too," I said. "Just try it without me. You have all you really need to play well."

And they did. In the practice they skated with confidence, a kind of "I'll show you" attitude that made me happy, even though it was me they were showing up.

As luck would have it, our very next game was against the Hurricanes. I'm sure Zack would have liked to play for the Rangers, but the Hurricanes were only one point behind us with four games left to play in the season. They had as good a shot as we did at the top spot. As Dad drove to the arena that evening, I felt weird knowing I would have to face Zack across the ice, like enemies.

"Dad," I said as we stopped at the light. "Who's your best friend?"

He seemed surprised by the question. "I don't know that I have one," he said thoughtfully. "What am I saying, you are, of course!"

"No, Dad," I went on. "Your adult best friend, I mean."

"Probably Sheldon then," he said after a moment.

"Do you ever fight with Sheldon?"

He laughed. "Not fist fights like you and Zack. We argue. That's the way adults fight." He added, "Usually."

"How do you make up?" I pressed him, wanting to know if he had some special techniques for ending a fight.

But he only shrugged and said, "Eventually you realize that it's silly to go on being mad, and there's nothing a man hates more than being silly." I thought about that as we drove the rest of the way to the arena.

The atmosphere in the dressing room was tense; I could feel it the moment I walked in. But Dad strode in behind me, full of confidence, and demanded everyone's attention.

"Kids, I know there's been some grumbling about this trade, but that's the way it is. You have a choice, you really do. You can grumble and forget all about how well you've played all season and the fact that a week ago you were on top. Or you can pull yourselves together and go out on that ice and claw your way back to the top, one goal at a time. I won't tell you which one to choose." Abruptly Dad left the room. We sat there, a bit startled. Fourteen pairs of eyes bore into me. Yeah, like it's all my fault, I thought. Suddenly I realized that my loser attitude was what Dad was talking about.

Softly I started chanting, "Win, win, win, win, win." At first I was alone, then Matt and Dustin joined in. Reluctantly the rest of the team took up the chant, and soon it swelled to fifteen shouting voices, mine the loudest of them all.

Taking up my equipment, I started dressing, holding each article up before I put it on. The team hurried to join me, each one picking up the old ritual. Dressed, I positioned myself beside the door. Natalie Plaxton presented her stick to me. I touched it solemnly, and all the rest as they filed by.

I'd be lying if I said I wasn't uncomfortable around Zack. Beside the odd sight of him in his Hurricane uniform, he had an attitude that put me off. Determined to say something, I skated toward him, but he swung away down the ice.

My jitters stopped the moment the puck was dropped. Moving confidently, I won the drop and shovelled the puck out to Erik. He was chased into the boards by Zack, who lost no time giving Erik a hard check. I took a run at Zack myself, knowing he would show no mercy, and true enough, he dusted me. It was a clean hit and play went on. Mark Levitt managed to snare a pass at centre ice, holding onto it long enough for me to catch up. "Mitch!" he cried out.

"Ready," I shouted back.

Mark fired it to Dustin waiting at the blue line. It went exactly as planned. Mark and I tore along after Dusty, who started a game of cat-and-mouse with the Hurricane defence on the point. Finally Erik lumbered into position, dropping the defending winger like a stone. The pass out missed him, heading straight for Zack's stick. I flew by, stealing it away. Only now I was perilously close to the blue line with a pack of Hurricane players on me, forcing me back. The good news was that a pack of Hurricanes at the blue line left precious few Hurricanes defending the net. And with the help of Johnny

Wolsky muscling them out of the way, I managed a half-hearted wrist shot in the direction of their goal. Dustin deflected it nicely, but their goalie kicked it back out. By now, the rest of the Hurricanes were howling down on us. I gritted my teeth and sent the rebound between the goalie's outstretched leg and his stick.

It was like old times out there, with heads butting, sticks waving and kids piling on me. I looked for Zack, but I couldn't see him. Not that I wanted to rub it in.

Our joy was short-lived, however. On a dumb penalty by Erik, Zack got his first goal of the night. Power-play goals should count for less, I thought, not for the first time. At least in points.

I passed Natalie on the change. "It's your night for a goal, Nat Plax," I shouted as she hurried by. She waved her stick in reply. Natalie hadn't scored a goal all season but was racking up a fair number of assists along the way.

Ian Rothenberg missed the face off, which luckily was in our end, because a big, dopey Hurricane winger went flying by in front of a rocketing slap shot aimed at our goal. The puck deflected off his skate and skimmed in the opposite direction. James Friesen got to it first but as he overskated it, his stick upended the puck and it wobbled feebly. Natalie hip-checked one of the biggest guys on the Hurricane team, much to his surprise, clearing the way for Ian to wake up and smell the rubber.

The big defenceman lumbered after Nat, and his slashing stick brought the play whistling to a halt. With a penalty to the other side, Dad sent my line back onto the ice to kill it. Natalie tore up to the bench. "Coach Stevens, I want to stay on," she said simply. He looked at her determined face and after a moment he nodded his assent. Grinning broadly, Natalie skated out, while an incredulous Erik was waved back to the bench.

"This is it, Nat," I called to her. "Keep your head up and your stick down."

Right from the face off, Nat stuck to the puck like glue. Everywhere it went, she was there. I caught up with her digging in the corner. "Nat," I hissed, "how can I set you up if I can't get the puck to pass to you?" Realization dawned on her face, and she backed away furiously, grinding into position in front of the net. When I finally got the puck out I only had room for a quick wrist shot. It found Nat standing guard, and quick as a wink she shovelled it under the goalie's pads. She had scored her first goal. I don't think I ever saw anybody that happy.

But once again, Zack showed us why he was a Pee Wee star. With fifteen seconds left in the penalty, he managed to break away and draw Matt out of the goal crease. The puck sailed into the net to the collective dismay of the Stingers.

Two minutes to play and we were deadlocked, two–two. Zack and I were both on the final shift.

I skated into position in the face-off circle. The Hurricane centre was getting antsy. He kept flicking his stick and putting it down, disrupting the face off. Finally, the ref waved him out of the circle. To my surprise, Zack waded in. For the first time ever, I faced my friend in a showdown. I don't know what he was thinking, but I was determined to score the winning goal. And I came close. The puck fell between our slashing sticks. I forced myself to concentrate on the puck, holding my breath until my stick connected, sending it over to Dustin in front of their net. We swatted around their goal, peppering the net with shots. We got every rebound, but one. The one that got away ended up on Zack's stick and we were faced with a wall of Hurricane players blocking our progress up the rink. Frustrated, we deked and wheeled about like crazy chickens, watching Zack move relentlessly toward Matt in our goal. Oh no, I thought. It's just like the last one, he'll fake him out and …

And then unexpectedly Zack dropped a pass back. The Hurricane winger took it smoothly, with all of us veering off on his tail. The shot on goal was right on target, if a little weak. Zack gave it a push, with Matt diving to block it a second too late. Zack's hat trick won them the game.

My teammates left the ice, dejected once more. I stayed behind and waited for the Hurricane to subside, leaving Zack alone. He eyed me warily, but this time he stayed put when I skated over to him. "Great play, Zack," I said, with my hand out to shake. It looked like he wasn't going to take it, but I persisted, hanging my hand out, waiting.

After what seemed like an hour, he shook it awkwardly. "Thanks," he said, his smile just beginning. "You too."

We kind of ran out of things to say then. So we skated off the ice together and went to our separate dressing rooms. My Dad had stood by, watching the whole thing.

"I think that went rather well," he said. "Don't you?"

11

Fast Friends

It was mid-March, and the weather was becoming awfully unpredictable, with some days getting up above freezing. Soon the season would end, the outdoor rinks would close and the only hockey we'd get would be on the TV. It seemed like ages since the day Zack and I vowed we'd win a spot at hockey camp. Every time I asked Dad about it, he brushed me off. Actually he said he didn't know who would be chosen, but I didn't believe him.

With the days getting longer, we had extra time to practise outdoors. As always, Matt and Dustin and I met after school at the rink near my house. Lately, Ian Rothenberg had been joining us for our pick-up games. Each time I went I hoped I'd see Zack, but since the trade he had never showed.

"Yo, buds," I saluted my friends, who were already on the benches by the rink, strapping on their blades.

"Rothenberg's coming after his mom gets home," Matt said.

"Any news about Zack?" I asked as casually as I could.

They shook their heads.

"All right, then, let's do it!" They followed me onto the ice.

Until Ian showed up, Dustin and I played one-on-one. We traded goals, giving Matt a real workout in the net. Finally Ian arrived and we took a break while he put on his skates. Then, out of nowhere, Zack appeared. Suddenly he was just standing there, staring at us over the fence.

"Hey, Zack!" Dusty cried. "Long time!"

Zack greeted the guys quietly.

Dusty continued, "Now we can play two-on-two."

I seized the opportunity by announcing, "Dustin and Ian against Zack and me. Okay?"

Everybody nodded in agreement. We waited a few moments longer for Zack to get ready.

Impatient to get going, I skated back on the ice, practising my backhand against the empty net. At last, the guys took to the ice, and Zack skated up beside me.

"Ready?"

It was the first time he'd spoken directly to me since he got there. He took a quarter out of his pocket and spun it high in the air. "Call it, Dusty," he cried.

"Heads!" The coin bounced and we chased it as it rolled down the ice, landing in the net. Dustin swooped down on it.

"Heads," he crowed triumphantly. "And the first goal is ours!"

Zack scooped the quarter off the ice, saying, "You wish."

"First team to score twenty-one goals wins," Matt called out. Zack and I took our positions defending the net while Ian and Dustin picked up the puck at the other end. Each pair had a run at the net with as many shots on goal as they could muster until the puck was snagged by Matt or cleared to the other end.

Dustin wasted no time flying in on net. He was a good player, and even though he didn't score as often as Zack and me, you still had to watch out for him. He flicked a neat backhander right over Zack's stick that sailed into the net behind Matt. "I'll write to you guys from Muskoka," he shouted.

On our first turn we were robbed by Matt, and I thought for a minute he'd let Dustin's shot through to lessen our advantage. But soon we were trading goal for goal as the score rose steadily. Finally we were tied, twenty apiece. It was already getting dark, and the rink lights cast pools of light and shadow that made it difficult to see the puck.

On Dusty and Ian's next try I picked off the rebound, sending it skidding into the net at the other end. The whole time we played, Zack barely said two words to me. But he played hard and looked pretty happy. We rounded up, facing down our opponents at the other end. "This is it," I said. Zack nodded, moving out, while I scooped the puck and started the drive. We passed back and forth a couple of times. Ian rushed Zack, thinking he would fire from the point, but Zack put on the brakes and lobbed it to me. Dustin didn't react fast enough to the new threat, and I spanked one over Matt's shoulder to win the competition.

Suddenly Zack was skating at me, with his head down, his stick swinging back and forth. Instinctively I lowered my head to accept his tribute. We cracked helmets and raised our sticks in triumph. Finally, we crossed swords and bowed to our friends.

It really was like old times, and all the anger and pride emptied out of me. "Dragonslayers!" I shouted.

"Dragonslayers triumph again!" Zack shouted back.

We collapsed onto the bench, laughing as though all the funny things in the world had happened to us in that one moment.

"Rats! I've missed dinner!" Ian sprang up, grabbed his gear and ran off into the night.

"Later, guys," Matt said. "C'mon Dustball, let's blow."

Dusty started to walk away with Matt, then turned back and addressed Zack, "I guess we won't be playing you again in the regular season. Good luck in the playoffs."

Zack nodded, but he made no move to get up, so I just stayed there on the bench with him. He seemed to want to say something, but couldn't get it out.

"They miss you on the team, Zack," I started. "I do too."

He was silent for a minute and finally broke into a big grin, saying, "At least it got you back on the A-line!"

I gave him a light punch in the shoulder. "Buzz off, Zack."

"Buzz off, Mitch."

We got up and headed for home.

"You know, I miss you guys too. I might even miss Natalie," Zack chuckled as we walked toward our houses. "But I can't exactly ask to be traded back," he added. "They'd be ticked off at me. I'd look like a real whiner."

I thought about that for a while. "I can ask Dad to arrange it. I'm sure he wants you back," I offered. We stopped at the corner where we usually parted. "Let me try," I said, seeing the doubt on his face.

"I'll look like a total idiot."

Laughing, I left him under the street light, saying over my shoulder, "Don't worry. I do it all the time. It works for me."

Seeing the van parked beside our house, I ran into the house shouting for my dad. "Hey, Dad," I cried. "Zack wants back on the team!" I just kept shouting until I found my father in the basement, changing the furnace filter. "Did you hear me? Zack wants to come back!"

My dad looked at me for a long moment, wiping his hands on a rag. I didn't like the look on his face. My spirits fell when he said, "Easier said than done." Where do parents get those goofy expressions?

12

Now Appearing at Centre Ice

Well, Dad did it. He wouldn't say how, but he got Zack back on our team for the final game of the season. But there was a price.

I checked my bag three times before we left the house. I even sniffed my jersey to make sure it was good and smelly. Last game and last chance to win, and even more important, last chance to show those invisible "scouts" that Zack and I deserved a shot at Muskoka.

At the arena, I greeted my friend with a grin. "Yo, Zack!"

"Yo, Mitch," he responded. "I feel a hat trick coming on."

We entered the dressing room together. Conversation dropped off as our teammates caught sight of Zack. It got pretty quiet for a moment. Then the room erupted in happy cheers as everyone gathered around to welcome Zack back to the Stingers. We dressed, then waited for Dad to come and give us our pep talk. I'd noticed that he liked to make a big entrance, waiting until just before ice time and then smacking the door open. Sure enough, the door banged open and he appeared with his clipboard.

"One change to the line-up — Zack Andermann is right wing, replacing Erik Swanson on the A-line." Zack and I grinned across the room at Dusty. "And Mitch Stevens has something to say to you." My dad turned to me.

I stood up. For once I was tongue-tied. "Um, yeah, I, um ..." I stammered. Taking a deep breath I carried on, "I just have to say, I mean I want to say, sorry for causing trouble on the team and stuff." I looked at my dad by the door.

"Is that okay?" I said to him. He leaned down and whispered a few words in my ear. "Oh yeah, I have to apologize for fighting. Fighting doesn't solve anything and I was wrong to, uh, umm, do it." I was sounding pretty dim, but I meant what I said. Dad nodded his approval. Relieved, I headed back to my seat. Johnny Wolsky buzzed softly. "Wait a minute," I shouted. "I almost forgot. I want to tell everybody — B-line and A-line — that I really respect their contribution to the team." Finally I sat down, pleased that I had managed to say the one thing that really needed to be said. I shot Johnny Wolsky a smug look.

"Okay everybody, that's it," Dad said. Zack and I looked at each other, confused, expecting a pep talk or something. Dad turned away, then stopped, adding, "No, wait, there is something else. Win!"

This time Matt started the chant, "Win, win, win, WIN!" We kept it up as the team filed out the door. I touched all the sticks and for a moment I was left alone in the dressing room. "Dragonslayers!" I whispered to myself.

I followed my team out onto the ice to face those pesky Rangers, who were our opponents in the final showdown. There I was again, face-to-face with my old opponent, MORG. With my new, improved attitude toward the world, I greeted her amiably, "Hey, what's your name?"

She ignored me.

"No seriously, I want to know. I'm Mitch, by the way." I stuck out my gloved hand. My smile seemed to loosen her up a bit.

Finally she spoke, but her voice was chilly. "My name is Morgan."

"No way!" I responded a little too loudly. I mean, what were the chances that MORG would turn out to be MORGan? The scowl returned to her face. I guess she thought I was making fun of her. And I didn't think she'd appreciate the joke if I explained it to her. So, we were sworn enemies once more, which was fine with me. I don't like to get too friendly with the competition before a game. You lose your edge.

Zack wasted no time getting started on his hat trick. His goal at two minutes into the game fired the team's spirit. Unfortunately, some of that energy made its way to the Rangers bench as they matched Zack's goal seven minutes later. A-line was red hot, with heads-up play and fabulous goaltending from Matt. Halfway through we were tied, two goals apiece. Both of ours were scored by Zack, assisted by you-know-who.

Only ten minutes to go and Zack fired one from the point that Dustin set up perfectly. It disappeared into the goalie. Not the net, the goalie. Zack raced in, poking around and waiting for it to come out before the ref whistled it down. I could hear the muffled cries of the Ranger goalie as Zack poked relentlessly. The ref had the whistle in his mouth, but the puck finally dribbled out. Triumphant, Zack pounced on it and fired it into the net for his hat trick. The team was on him before we could butt heads, but it was okay with me. We were ahead again.

We left the ice at the end of our shift. Dad grabbed me before I could sit down. "How do you feel about taking the B-line for a while?"

"Why?" I asked, surprised.

"They could use your help. A-line can hold their own. You think about it." And he walked away. I had a few minutes to watch the B-line and ponder. They were playing great defensively, but Dad was right, their offence was disorganized. A one-goal lead didn't mean much with the Rangers. If they scored again, maybe I should stay on the A-line. It was a tough decision. I wished Dad would just tell me what to do, instead of giving me a choice. Their shift ended and I shuffled to the end of the bench for the change. At the last moment I made up my mind. I would skate with the B-line. I sat down again and nodded to my dad. He sent Rothenberg back on the ice.

I didn't mind the extra rest, and when our turn came we were still ahead. The clock ran down relentlessly, and at five minutes, with our lead holding, the team seemed to relax a bit. Mistake! Wolsky let a Ranger fake him out and the next thing we knew the Rangers ace scorer had *his* hat trick and a tied game.

Dad looked upset, and I suspected he wanted to let the A-line stay out for another shift, but they needed the rest. So out went the B-line. "We don't leave the ice without a goal. Hear me?" I ordered. My linemates nodded fiercely. We were working hard, and we covered more ice than Antarctica, but time was running out and we couldn't even get a decent shot on the net.

With thirty seconds to go and the face off in our end, I wanted to win it and carry the puck myself. But the Ranger centre took it. Furious, I chased it down, stealing a pass. It was the break I needed. "Plax," I yelled. Natalie looked alertly at me, poised to receive my pass. Taking it cleanly, she broke for the blue line, with every player on the ice on her tail. She crossed inches ahead of me, and with Levitt and Friesen protecting her back, passed it to me as I streaked by. Break-away!

Heart pounding and legs pumping, I took a run straight at the net. I could see the surprise on the goalie's face when he realized I wasn't going to stop. Fully expecting to let the boards stop me, I veered around the net, deftly transferring the puck from the front to the back of my stick. I let out a howl as I streaked past the net, backhanding the puck through the opening the wide-eyed goalie left me. With a crash I hit the boards, falling back onto the ice. Raising my stick in triumph, the rest of my B-liners fell on me.

For the last few seconds of the game, I felt like I was floating on air. When the buzzer finally went every Stinger spilled onto the ice, led by Zack in his characteristic head-down approach. The Dragonslayers ended the season in a blaze of glory.

Zack ended our routine and paused a moment before skating over to James and Natalie. He clapped Nat on the back and reached up to high-five James. Together we skated over to shake with our opponents.

After the handshaking at centre ice was over, we headed for the dressing rooms. Zack waited at the gate. "Do it, Mitch. You earned it," he said with a smile. I stepped back onto the ice for my star turn as Zack announced dramatically, "The First Star, Mitch Stevens!" Making my circle, I swung my stick over my helmet with both hands, narrowly missing Zack's head.

"Your turn," I said.

"Nah. I'll wait for the interviews in the dressing room."

A sticky spray of ginger ale greeted us as we entered. Kids and equipment were piled everywhere, but the parents were staying clear in the shower area. My mom, my sister and Mr. and Mrs. Andermann were all in there laughing along with everyone else. I thought I'd caught a glimpse of my dad, but when I looked closer I could see he wasn't there.

Natalie came up to me grinning widely. "That was awesome, Mitch," she said.

"Yeah, thanks, Nat." We stood there awkwardly and then she shrugged, turning to go. "Hey Nat!" I shouted. "You were pretty awesome too."

She gave me two thumbs up. I went to sit down beside Zack and pull off my gooey gear. Kids were still whooping and hollering, Matt and Dustin in the thick of it. Just like before the game, the door banged open and there was Dad. His whistle echoed in the small room, silencing the pack of us.

"I just want to say that I think you're the best bunch of hockey players in the city of Toronto, and it's been an honour to serve as your coach. Congratulations to all of you," he said solemnly. The whooping started again, but apparently he wasn't finished. The whistle blasted one more time.

"For twenty-five kids in our league the season's not over yet. And two of them are right here on our team." Zack and I looked at each other, almost afraid to hear him finish. "Zack Andermann and Mitch Stevens ... you're going to Muskoka!"

I'm still smiling.